The Stepmother

Drizella

The Fairy Godmother

Anastasia

The Baker

Published by Hachette Partworks Ltd
ISBN: 978-1-906965-59-4
Date of Printing: May 2011
Printed in Singapore by Tien Wah Press

"Come on Gus-Gus. Faster!" urged Jaq.

"What's the hurry?" wondered Gus as he raced out of the mouse hole after his friend.

"Fairy Godmother's here!" Jaq explained. "She is reading the story of Cinderella to everyone in the library."

Gus and Jaq arrived at the library in time to hear the Fairy Godmother read, "Cinderella and the Prince lived happily ever after. The end!"

Gus was very disappointed to have missed the story. "Aw, maybe you could read another one?" he asked.

The Fairy Godmother shook her head. "I'm sorry, Gus, but that's the only Cinderella book there is."

Then Gus had an idea...

"Maybe we could make another book," Gus suggested.

Most of the other mice cheered. But not Jaq.

"No, no. Who would read a book made by mice?" worried the thin little mouse.

"Cinderella would love to read it," said the Fairy Godmother. Then she waved her magic wand.

Poof! A book cover and paper appeared. The mice and birds set to work. They decorated the cover and sewed the pages into it with a needle and thread. But something was still missing – the stories!

The mice knew some good stories. There was the one about Cinderella's first day in the castle. And another about the time Jaq was human for a day. They put these in the book.

"Why don't we tell the story of Anastasia falling in love?" Gus offered.

That surprised the Fairy Godmother. "Anastasia? Cinderella's stepsister? That Anastasia?"

"Yes," the mice agreed. Then they told the Fairy Godmother the story of... *An Uncommon Romance.*

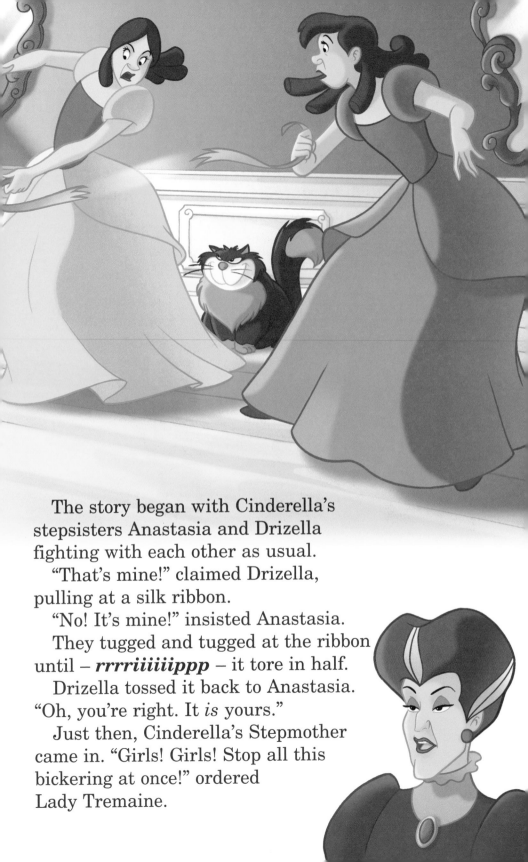

The story began with Cinderella's
stepsisters Anastasia and Drizella
fighting with each other as usual.

"That's mine!" claimed Drizella,
pulling at a silk ribbon.

"No! It's mine!" insisted Anastasia.

They tugged and tugged at the ribbon
until – *rrrriiiiiippp* – it tore in half.

Drizella tossed it back to Anastasia.
"Oh, you're right. It *is* yours."

Just then, Cinderella's Stepmother
came in. "Girls! Girls! Stop all this
bickering at once!" ordered
Lady Tremaine.

"Cinderella's ball is tomorrow night, so pay attention!" their mother commanded. "Every noble bachelor in the kingdom will be there! To find a husband, you must make the most of this opportunity!"

Lady Tremaine continued, "A perfect appearance is how to catch a proper gentleman. We shall find you men of wealth and nobility."

Anastasia became excited. "Maybe a count!"

"Or a duke!" Drizella added. They both began
frantically putting on perfumes and powders.

Of course, Anastasia and Drizella needed new
gowns and new shoes for the ball. "The fancier
the better!" declared Lady Tremaine. So they set
off for the village market.

Cinderella was also on her way to the market. The princess had slipped out of the castle wearing an old dress so that no one would notice her.

But that didn't fool her friends the birds and the mice. "Morning, Cinderelly!" they called when they spotted her.

Cinderella put her finger to her lips to hush them. "I want to surprise the Prince with a garland of flowers," she explained.

She invited her friends to come along. So Jaq and Gus hopped into her basket.

Anastasia, Drizella and their mother arrived in the Market Square. Anastasia watched as the flower man sold a garland of flowers to a young couple.

"Remember the tradition! Give these to each other at the ball, and you'll always be together!" he said.

The flower man spotted Anastasia. "Need a garland of roses for the ball?"

Anastasia reached for the flowers.

"Anastasia! What are you doing?" her mother scowled.

The young woman jerked her hand away and left. Then, as she neared the bakery, the smell of baking bread drew her inside.

She found herself right in front of the Baker. Their eyes met. He smiled and offered her a fresh roll. Anastasia shyly accepted the gift.

Cinderella was passing by and saw all this through the window.

Suddenly Lady Tremaine stormed in and snatched the roll from Anastasia. "I think not. Everything in this shop is... inferior."

"You could build a house out of these bricks," Drizella added, tossing a roll aside.

Cinderella watched, unnoticed, as Lady Tremaine dragged Anastasia out of the shop and hissed, "You're not to say a word to that... shopkeeper. I forbid it!"

Cinderella explained to her friends, "I know that look! I think they're in love!"

Jaq looked at her, laughing. "Anastasia's in love? That's crazy, Cinderelly!"

But Cinderella knew better. "Anyone can fall in love!"

"Heh! Anyone but Anastasia," the mice giggled.

"She just needs some help," Cinderella said softly.
"I had lots of help, too. Remember?"

Jaq and Gus certainly did. They had helped her to
meet the Prince! They agreed to help Anastasia and
the Baker. But how?

"I know! We'll lure them into the square," said
Cinderella. Then she whispered the rest of her plan
to her friends.

To carry out the plan, the bluebirds swooped down and snatched Anastasia's bonnet, carrying it out of her reach.

"Outta my way," Anastasia yelled as she clumsily chased the birds. She shoved her way through the stalls and carts, causing everything to tip and spill.

Gus and Jaq led the other mice into the
bakery. The mice tried to get the Baker's
attention, but nothing worked. The Baker just
didn't notice them.

So Cinderella leaned around the door and whistled sharply!

The Baker whirled around. "Mice!" he shouted.

The Baker began chasing the mice out of his shop.

Meanwhile, the birds dropped Anastasia's bonnet in front of the bakery.

Anastasia rushed over, picked it up, and jammed it on her head. As she turned to storm off she ran straight into the Baker!

But before the two could speak, Gus dashed between a horse's legs and spooked the horse.

The startled horse kicked
out in fright, accidentally
striking Anastasia. She
flew through the air, past
the startled Baker, and
landed...

... on some eggs! Anastasia was a
mess! She was so embarrassed that
she ran from the bakery, crying.

Anastasia ran through the market. Everyone laughed at the young woman.

But Cinderella felt horrible! This wasn't how she had planned it at all.

Cinderella and her friends found Anastasia. "I
saw you in the Baker's shop," Cinderella said gently.
Anastasia groaned, "He must think I'm... *ugh*."
Cinderella shook her head. "He saw it was an
accident! Don't give up so fast."

"I'll help you," Cinderella continued. "Come back to the castle, and we'll clean you up. Then we'll get you two together."

"But Mother forbids it! She thinks he's beneath me," replied Anastasia.

Cinderella smiled. "I think she's wrong. The Baker's terrific. And you'll never go hungry!" she added.

Cinderella and Anastasia returned to the castle.

Cinderella cleaned up her stepsister's face. "There. Good as new."

"Don't stop now! Mother says that looks count for everything!"

Cinderella disagreed. "You want to look your best, but that isn't the most important thing."

"You're right, what I need is a whole new look!" said Anastasia, not understanding Cinderella's words.

They got to
work. Cinderella
gave Anastasia
a dress and
necklace to wear.

Anastasia admired
herself in the mirror. She
couldn't believe it was her!
Cinderella then gave
her some advice. "Just
remember, you'll catch
more flies with honey than
with vinegar."
"Who'd want to
catch flies?" wondered
Anastasia. She obviously
didn't understand
Cinderella's message.

Cinderella patiently explained, "The best way
to impress the Baker is to be nice. You could
start with a smile."

But Anastasia even needed help smiling!

At last, Anastasia was ready to meet the
Baker again.

"He'll never be able to resist," Cinderella
promised.

Anastasia was still worried. "But Mother told me never to speak to the Baker again," she said.

Cinderella took her stepsister's hand. "Maybe it's time to stop following somebody else's orders... and start following your heart. Meet me in the market at noon tomorrow and we will walk to the bakery."

Anastasia was so excited. "I can hardly wait!"

The next morning, Anastasia needed an excuse to go to the bakery. She snatched up all the bread and threw it outside. Then she hurried to the carriage, calling, "Mother! I have to run to town! We're out of bread!"

In the market, the Baker had bought a garland of flowers from the flower man.

Shortly afterwards, Anastasia bought an identical garland!

Cinderella joined her stepsister in the market. With a few encouraging words from Cinderella, Anastasia went off to see the Baker.

But as Anastasia neared the bakery, she saw the Baker holding a garland of flowers and talking to a pretty woman! Anastasia's heart was broken!

Anastasia left before she could see the pretty woman's husband walk out of the bakery!

Instead, hurt and upset, Anastasia raced off, tossing her own flowers away!

The Baker spotted Anastasia and dashed off after her. He had truly bought the flower garland for her!

He searched the market, but he couldn't find her anywhere. Where could she be?

Anastasia ran past Cinderella, crying! Cinderella
tried to follow her, but just then, a speeding carriage
blocked Cinderella's path!

After the carriage had
passed, Anastasia was
nowhere to be seen!

The tired Baker sat down to rest. He didn't notice that a goat had begun to eat his garland until it was too late. The Baker was able to save only a single flower.

Just then the Baker heard someone sniffing. He turned and saw Anastasia! "Don't look at me! I look horrible!" she cried, ready to run again.

But the Baker didn't think so at all. "Wait! Please! Don't run away!" He held out the single flower. Anastasia took it and smiled!

To the Baker, it was the most beautiful smile in the world.

Suddenly Drizella and Lady Tremaine pounced upon them. "Anastasia! You were forbidden to speak to this man!" Lady Tremaine said. Drizella snickered.

Her mother grabbed Anastasia's arm and said, "Come along!"

But Anastasia pulled her arm free and grabbed the Baker's hand. "No, Mother! You're wrong. He's sweet."

"She's wonderful," the Baker added, looking at Anastasia.

Anastasia looked at her astonished mother and declared, "We are going to the ball together!"

Lady Tremaine left in a huff, dragging Drizella with her.

The Baker took Anastasia's hand. Cinderella let out a sigh of relief.

So Anastasia and the Baker went to the ball.

As Cinderella and her Prince waltzed beside
them, Anastasia whispered to Cinderella,
"I'm so happy! I can't believe this! I'm so...
I'm... I'm so..."

Cinderella smiled at her. "I know! Me too!"
she said.

"And that is the story of how Anastasia fell in love," Gus finished.

"Perfect!" cried Jaq, closing the book. The Fairy Godmother smiled proudly.

The mice scurried out to give Cinderella her gift.

Cinderella loved the book her friends had made for her. Soon they were all sitting together in the library.

The mice listened eagerly as Cinderella began to read. "Once upon a time, there was a big castle..."